Bedtime Tales includes:

Said The Kitty To The Cat...

Milly the Meerkat

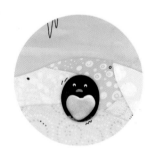

Little Penguin
Learns to swim

Bedtime on the Farm

Hiku

Hic!

Cub's First Winter

The Silent Owl

Said The Kitty To The Cat...

Written by Vincent Spada Illustrated by Steve Whitlow

On a couch was a cat,
with the cat was a kitty.
So cute, with a bow,
sitting there, looking pretty.

On the couch was a box
full of sweets, itty-bitty.
Still sealed. Oh no!
What a shame, what a pity!

'Let's open them up,
for they look so pretty,'
said the kitty to the cat,
said the cat to the kitty.

'But the box is sealed!
What a shame, what a pity!'
said the kitty to the cat,
said the cat to the kitty.

'Let's ask the bird,'
said the cat to the kitty.
'She can open the box!
She has a beak so pretty!'

But the bird was asleep!
What a shame, what a pity!
Said the kitty to the cat,
Said the cat to the kitty.

'I guess we can't have them,
those sweets, itty-bitty,'
said the kitty to the cat,
said the cat to the kitty.

But then they heard a noise
outside, and a ditty.
Their owner had come home,
from her shopping in the city!

When their owner came inside,
from her shopping in the city,
they asked her for the sweets,
sitting there, looking pretty.

'Of course,' said their owner,
to her cat and her kitty.
'Those sweets are for you!
I bought them in the city.'

Then they thanked their owner,
giving kisses, itty-bitty,
for the sweets that she'd bought
on her visit to the city.

And soon, it was bedtime.
What a shame, what a pity!
But the day had been fun
for the cat and the kitty.

'Goodnight, and sleep tight.
I love you, little pretty,'
said the kitty to the cat ...

... said the cat to the kitty.

Milly the Meerkat

Written by Oakley Graham
Illustrated by Alexia Orkrania

For Noah

There once was a young meerkat called Milly, who was bored as she stood on an earth mound taking her turn as lookout.

To amuse herself, Milly took a great, big breath and barked out, 'Snake! Snake! A snake is approaching the baby meerkats' burrow!'

All the other meerkats came running out of their own burrows to help Milly drive the snake away.

But when they arrived at the top of the mound, they found no snake. Milly laughed at the sight of their angry faces.

'Don't bark "snake", Milly,'
said the other meerkats,
'if there's no snake!'

Late in the afternoon,
Milly saw a REAL
snake slithering
close to the baby
meerkats' burrow.

Alarmed, Milly leapt to her feet and barked out as loudly as she could, 'Snake! Snake! A snake is approaching the baby meerkats' burrow!'

But the other meerkats just thought that Milly was trying to fool them again, so they didn't come out to help her.

Outside, as day turned to night, everyone wondered why Milly hadn't returned for supper. They went to look for Milly and found her crying on top of the lookout mound.

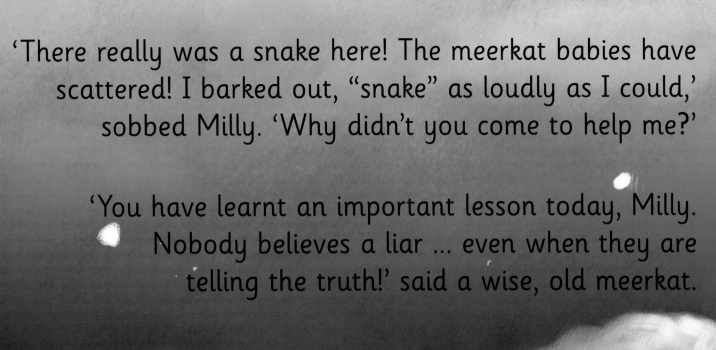

'There really was a snake here! The meerkat babies have scattered! I barked out, "snake" as loudly as I could,' sobbed Milly. 'Why didn't you come to help me?'

'You have learnt an important lesson today, Milly. Nobody believes a liar ... even when they are telling the truth!' said a wise, old meerkat.

The entire meerkat colony helped Milly look for the lost babies and once they were all found, they tucked them up safely in their burrows.

Milly was very sorry for what she had done and promised that she would never lie to her family and friends again.

Little Penguin
Learns to Swim

Written by Eilidh Rose

Illustrated by Dubravka Kolanovic

It was an important day for Little Penguin.
He was going swimming for the very first time.

Little Penguin was nervous about learning to swim,
but he wanted to splash and play with his friends.
So he started to slowly waddle along the icy
path towards the big, blue ocean.

Little Penguin was shuffling through the snow,
practising flapping his flippers and wiggling his feet,
when he saw Little Bird hopping towards him.

'I'm learning to fly!' said Little Bird.

'Are you scared?' asked Little Penguin.

'Not really. I'm not very good yet, but I can almost get off the ground,' said Little Bird proudly.

Little Penguin continued down the icy path to the ocean.
Suddenly, he saw a black shadow on the fluffy white
snow. High above him in the bright blue sky was
Little Bird, twirling and swooping through the air.

'I'm finally flying!' Little Bird
squawked happily.

As he was practising wiggling his feet,
Little Penguin heard a splash and Little Seal
jumped up on the ice beside him.

'I'm learning to fish!'
said Little Seal, happily.

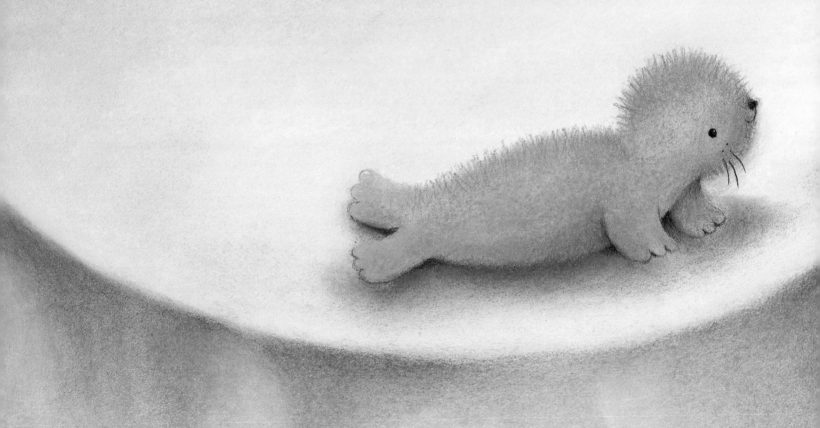

'Are you nervous?' asked Little Penguin.

'Not really. I haven't caught anything yet, but it's lots of fun!'

Little Seal saw a school of fish swimming past, so she quickly plunged back into the water.

Waddling on, Little Penguin heard
a big splash and an excited shout.

'Look, Little Penguin!'
cried Little Seal. 'I caught a fish!'
Little Seal whizzed off to show all of her other friends.

Little Penguin waddled to the edge
and looked down into the deep, dark water.
It looked very cold and he didn't want to go in.
But then he thought about his friends and how
they were not scared to learn new things.

Little Penguin shuffled closer and,
with a deep breath, slid on his
tummy and slipped easily into the water.
Just like he had practised, Little Penguin
flapped his flippers and wiggled his feet,
twirling and twisting through the water.

Little Penguin whizzed over to his
friends to join in with their games.
Even though he had been nervous before,
Little Penguin could not wait to come
back for more fun tomorrow!

Bedtime on the Farm

Written by Corinne Mellor
Illustrated by Karen Sapp

Farmer Jack stands with his dog by the gate,
He looks at the sky – it's getting quite late.
'Time to get everyone back home for bed,
Let's round them up and then get them all fed.'

'I need my dog's help,' says old Farmer Jack.
'His name is Fred and he helps lead the pack.'
High up in the tree, two small kittens mew,
'Jump down,' says Jack, 'the line starts with you!'

Can you count one dog and two kittens by the farm gate?

They come to a field where Fred stops and pauses.
There eating the grass are three pretty horses.
'Come join us,' Jack says. 'Please get into line,
This journey back home could take us some time!'

Can you count three pretty horses in the field?

They all follow Jack; the kittens are mewing,
To a field full of flowers where four cows are chewing.
Fred looks at the cows and then starts to bark,
'We've got to go home – it's getting quite dark!'

Can you count four cows in the meadow?

They walk in a line along a small track,
Jack and Fred lead with the cows at the back.
Then up a small hill that's not very steep,
They collect Jack's five fluffy sheep.

Can you count five fluffy sheep
on the hillside?

At the top of the hill, where the green grass gets thinner,
Six billy goats are all eating their dinner.
'Let's get you home and give you some hay,'
Says Jack to the goats as he leads the way.

Can you count six billy goats on the hill?

They all tread downhill as the light starts to dim,
To a river where ducks and fish like to swim.
Jack's seven ducks are splashing about,
'Come on, quacking ducks
– it's time to get out!'

Can you count seven ducks around the river?

They follow the river along a small path,
Where eight muddy pigs are having a bath.
Farmer Jack frowns before shaking his head,
'I'll clean you all up before going to bed!'

Can you count eight pigs on the muddy bank?

All of the animals come to a stop.
They've reached a hill with nine hens at the top.
'Come on, little hens, not far to go!'
Jack says as he spies the farmyard below.

Can you count nine hens on the hill?

At last! The creatures arrive at the yard,
It's been a long walk, and they're very tired.
And although it's near the end of the day,
There are ten little mice still hard at play.
Can you count ten mice in the yard?

It's bedtime on the farm, so why don't you look,
And count all the animals that you met in this book?

Hiku

By Nicole Snitselaar and Coralie Saudo

Hiku, a little penguin, was feeling grumpy one morning.

It was one of those days, when the ice was too bright,
the sun was too hot, and his mummy woke him up too early.
'Don't forget that all of our family are visiting today!'
she reminded him.

Oh no! A family visit was the
last thing Hiku wanted! Smiling, greeting,
being polite and listening to, 'You look so
cute with your white heart-shaped tummy!' all day.

Soon, Hiku saw his family arriving, some by sea, some over the ice field. Hiku slipped past without being noticed and waddled to his hiding place. 'At last!' he whispered with relief, snuggling into his special snow hole.

'It's so nice to have some peace and quiet,' thought Hiku.
But, very soon he grew bored and lonely.
Sitting in his hiding place, Hiku started to think of some happy times
that he had spent with his family.

That wonderful day at the swimming pool ...
sliding, playing, splashing, getting soaked!

Diving deep underwater,
searching for lost treasures.

That time, when full of wonder, Hiku and his family huddled together, watching the Southern Lights.

And those evenings in front of the blazing fire ... grilling fish and listening to scary stories.

'Oh, what fun my family and I have together,' sighed Hiku.
'What am I doing here all by myself?
I hope it's not too late ...'
And, without a second thought, Hiku waddled back to join his family.

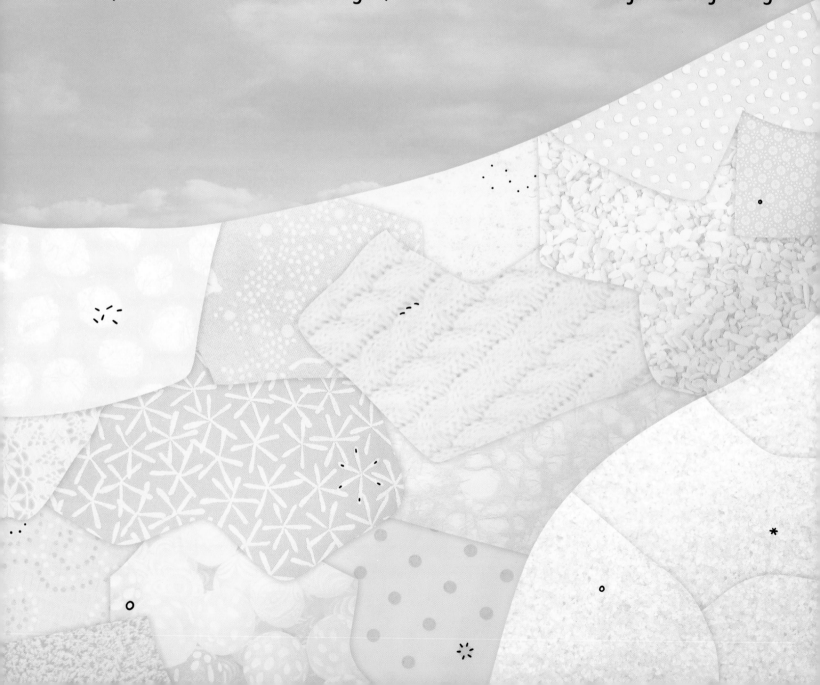

Hiku arrived just in time for the family photo!

'Ready? 1, 2, 3 … Hiku!' said the photographer.
'Hiku, Hiku, say cheese or you'll freeze!' laughed everyone.

And Hiku joined in with the
family fun and games.

Hic!

Written by Jaclin Azoulay
Illustrated by Alexia Orkrania

For my mum Pat, my dad Angelo, my Uncle Owen,
Raz, Inbar, Gai, Daniel, Lia and Oded. With love always.

Snuffletrump the piglet was sad.
Everyone seemed to have forgotten it was
his birthday today. No cards, no presents,
just … '**Hic!**' – the hiccups.

Mummy Pig and Daddy
Pig were very busy.
When Snuffletrump asked
if he could help, all that
came out was, '**Hic!**'
'Oink! You go off and play!'
Daddy Pig told Snuffletrump.

Cow told Snuffletrump that the only cure for hiccups was to drink a glass of her milk whilst standing on your head ... but it didn't help. '**Hic!**'

Poor Snuffletrump! Now he had the hiccups, no happy birthday, and milk all over him!
'**Hic!** Thank you for trying to help, Cow,' he said.

Over at the hen house the naughty, pecky, gossipy hens laughed, 'Bok, bok, bok, bok, bok!' when they heard Snuffletrump's hiccups. '**Hic!**'
'Everyone knows what you cock-a-doodle-do to cure the hiccups!' said Rooster, with a glint in his eye. 'You must juggle some eggs!'

Snuffletrump wasn't so sure, but he didn't want to be rude. He started to juggle the eggs. Splat! Splat! Splat! '**Hic!**' Snuffletrump now had hiccups, no happy birthday, milk all down his face, and egg on his head too!

Snuffletrump didn't feel like saying anything to those mean old hens, but he remembered his manners. '**Hic!** Thank you for trying to help,' he said.

Duck quacked at Snuffletrump from the pond, where she was teaching her ducklings to swim.
'Oh, Snuffletrump!' she said. 'I heard your hiccups from over here! You frightened my ducklings! Quack!'
'Sorry, Duck. **Hic!**' said Snuffletrump.

'Don't you know that the surest cure for
hiccups is a splash of cold water?' Duck said.
With that, Duck and all of her ducklings started
splishing and splashing Snuffletrump.

When they had stopped splashing, Snuffletrump
stood and waited. Duck and her ducklings waited.
'Oh!' Snuffletrump said, at last, with a smile.
'I'm clean again! Thank you Duck, thank you ducklings!
My hiccups have …

Hic! … still not gone.'
Snuffletrump was clean, but he still had no
happy birthday, and he still had the hiccups!

Then Snuffletrump saw Mummy Pig and
Daddy Pig waving to him from the barn, so
he headed over there as fast as he could.

'HAPPY BIRTHDAY SNUFFLETRUMP!'
Mummy Pig and Daddy Pig and all of
Snuffletrump's friends were in the barn with the
biggest birthday party he had ever seen!

Snuffletrump found
out what the nicest possible
cure for hiccups is ... a surprise!

Cub's First Winter

by Rebecca Elliott

'For Mum and Dad who have always taken such
good care of their own cubs. x'

It was the first day of winter
and Cub could not sleep. 'OK,' said Mum.
'One more forest walk before bed. Come on ...'

'Why are all the trees undressed?' asked Cub.

'So that we can have
fun in the leaves!'
answered Mum.

And the snow clouds
gathered in the sky.

'Why are my friends asleep
all the time?' asked Cub.
'Ssshhh! So that we can
laugh at their snoring!'
giggled Mum.

And the first snowflake
fell to the ground.

'Why are the birds
going on holiday?' asked Cub.
'So they can tell us all about their
journey when they come back!' said Mum.

And the snow began to gently fall.

'Why is it so windy?' asked Cub.
'So that we can be blown about together
in the tall grass!' laughed Mum.

And the snow drifted down.

'Why can I see my own breath?' asked Cub.
'So that we can puff like steam trains!' puffed Mum.

And the snow began to settle on the ground.

'Why is the river solid?' asked Cub.
'So that we can slide and dance on it!' exclaimed Mum.

And the snow fell more quickly.

'Why does the sun disappear
so early?' asked Cub.
'So that we can look up
at the stars for longer,'
explained Mum.

And the snow got
deeper and deeper.

'Why is everything white?' asked Cub.

'Oh no!' gasped Mum.
'Quick, follow me before we lose our way home!'

And back they went through the white forest,
over the white river, up and down the white rocks and
round and round the white trees until,
at last, they found their way home!

'Why is it so c-c-cold?'
asked Cub.

'So that we can snuggle up tight,' whispered Mum, with a smile.

'Why am I so tired?'
yawned Cub.
'Because it is sleepy time,'
murmured Mum.
'Night, night little cub.'

The Silent Owl

Written by Clemency Pearce
Illustrated by Sam McPhillips

For Rob and Silkie - Sam
For Gemma, the noisiest bird I know - CP

In the great old hollow oak,
Lived an owl, who never spoke.

Fox asked, 'Why do you never speak?'
But Owl refused to move his beak.

Badger huffed, 'How very rude!'
But Owl would not, could not, be moved!

A swooping bat whooped, 'Say hello!'

But Owl was silent far below.

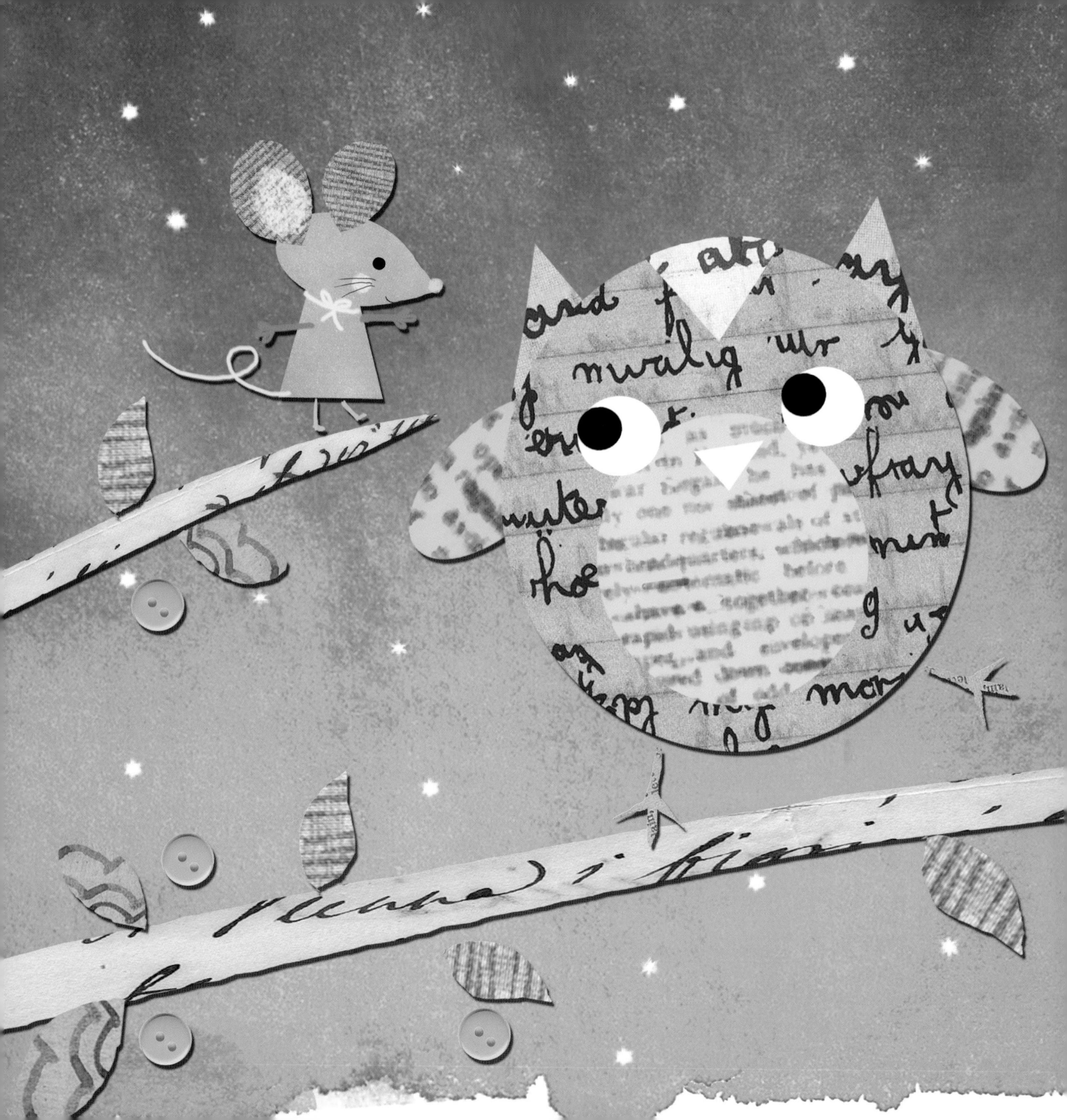

A pair of mice squeaked in his ear,
'Is it that you cannot hear?'
But Owl just rolled his giant eyes,
And stared up at the starry skies.

Squirrel scolded, 'Are you nuts?'
But Owl ignored his toothy tuts.

Rat cried, 'Owl! This isn't right!'
But Owl just gazed into the night.

Stag said, 'Owl! We need a sign,
To let us know that you are fine.'

So all the creatures gathered round,
To see if Owl would make a sound.

They stared at Owl; he stared right back.
Who would be the first to crack?

Stag declared,
'He must be mute,
Or he doesn't give
a hoot!'

At this, the owl produced a trumpet,
A big bass drum and stick to thump it.

Although Owl wouldn't hoot,
he played the bongos,

piano,

guitar,

and flute!

The animals cheered, 'What a clever bird!'
And Owl just winked without a word.